MARLIE'S AWAKENING

Amish Romance

HANNAH MILLER

Tica House
Publishing

Sweet Romance that Delights and Enchants!

Copyright © 2019 by Tica House Publishing LLC

All rights reserved.

No part of this book may be reproduced in any form or by any electronic or mechanical means, including information storage and retrieval systems, without written permission from the author, except for the use of brief quotations in a book review.

Personal Word from the Author

To My Dear Readers,

How exciting that you have chosen one of my books to read. Thank you! I am proud to now be part of the team of writers at Tica House Publishing who work joyfully to bring you stories of hope, faith, courage, and love.

Please feel free to contact me as I love to hear from my readers. I would like to personally invite you to sign up for updates and to become part of our **Exclusive Reader Club** —it's completely Free to join! Hope to see you there!

With love,

Hannah Miller

VISIT HERE to Join our Reader's Club and to Receive Tica House Updates:

http://ticahousepublishing.subscribemenow.com

Chapter One

Marlie cringed as she watched Grant head for the front door. The divorce papers had been signed days before, and now he was taking the last of his possessions from the house.

He stopped and turned to her. "I want you out of here in two days. The house is mine, and I'm gonna sell it. And as for this pregnancy of yours...? Do whatever you want, but leave me out of it." His tone mocked her. "Good luck finding somewhere to go."

He put his hand on the doorknob, gave her one last snort, and turned to go. Marlie's shoulders slumped as she realized just how final this was.

"I *have* friends, you know," she whispered to his retreating back.

He stopped to face her again.

"You? Friends? They're *my* friends," he scoffed. "They never could stand you. I'm surprised you didn't figure that out." He let out a satisfied laugh.

"You don't know that," Marlie countered. "I have friends."

"Yeah, right. You're completely cut off. Not even your family cares if you live or die, remember?"

Anger surged through her, and she squared her shoulders. "I'll be fine," she retorted, trying to muster her faltering courage.

"Oh, I doubt that. Remember, two days, or I will own everything you have." He was clearly enjoying this—clearly enjoying threatening her one last time before he left for good.

The door slammed behind him.

Two days wasn't a lot of time to move her entire life. Marlie squeezed her eyes shut for a brief moment. She would leave the city. Living there had only brought her grief and heartache. Leaving would give her a chance to start over with new people in a new place.

Hopefully, Grant wouldn't follow her. But then, why would he? He'd quite literally slammed the door on them as a couple. He'd falsely claimed in court that she'd been unfaithful, so what would be his purpose in following her anywhere? Yet, she didn't trust anything about him—not anymore.

She wondered if she was turning paranoid.

She walked over to her laptop. She sat down and started looking up places to go in Indiana. She couldn't travel far, for she had very little money. Due to his trumped-up accusations of infidelity, Grant and his fancy lawyers had figured out a way to leave her with no assets.

Marlie spotted a little town called Baker's Corner on the map. She raised an eyebrow. She'd never heard of the place, but it had a nice sound to it. Her next step was finding out everything she could about the place. Baker's Corner turned out to be mainly an Amish community, and it looked absolutely beautiful in the online pictures posted by visitors and tourists.

Marlie had always found the Amish intriguing. Over the years, she'd heard things here and there about their lifestyle, and she was curious. A complete cleanse from the world she had known could be helpful. Moving to an Amish community might be just what she needed to begin anew.

Marlie made a quick decision. Baker's Corner it would be.

With that, she set about packing what she thought she might need in her only suitcase. When that was full, she started hauling her remaining belongings to the thrift shop just down the street. She wouldn't need to take any of it with her to Baker's Corner.

However, she didn't take her extra clothing to the thrift shop. Marlie had an impressive array of elegant garments and accessories, for Grant had wanted her to appear like the perfect housewife in the home and the perfect trophy wife when they went out. Marlie took those outfits to the consignment shop in her neighborhood.

She set her first load on the counter. "Here are some of the things I have for you today."

The woman behind the counter gave her a friendly smile. She eyed the clothing. "Hmm. Let me go through these, and I'll determine how much I can give you for them. We tend to take only the more elite, high-end brands, but we pay well."

"All right. Thank you."

With that, Marlie stood back to let the woman look through the clothes she had brought.

"These are amazing brands. Is this all you have right now?" the woman questioned her. Marlie shook her head.

"I have more to bring. Do you want to wait and see everything all at once, or pay by the batch?"

"We'll do it batch by batch. That'll make it easier," the woman decided.

So, that was what they did. Marlie waited patiently while the woman went through each group of clothing. What the woman didn't take – which was very little – Marlie took to the thrift shop before she returned to repeat the process. It made her a decent amount of money, hopefully enough to make her move to the Amish community of Baker's Corner.

After Marlie disposed of all of her belongings, she took her suitcase from the bedroom. She tucked her cell phone into her purse, and her laptop sat snugly inside her suitcase. Just because she was moving to an Amish area didn't necessarily mean that she would be living like them with no technology.

Marlie made the trip to Baker's Corner by rideshare apps. Most wouldn't take her all the way to the community, but she finally found one who would, for a fraction of what the others were asking.

"Thank you," Marlie said gratefully as the last driver let her off.

"I hope you enjoy being here with the Amish folks. They're not a bad sort of people," he mused. "Fact is, they're right nice. I've met a few over the years."

"Here you are." Marlie offered up the fare. He took her money, counted it, and then returned a portion of it to her.

She frowned in confusion. "I thought you asked for—"

"Keep it," he said, interrupting her. "I'm thinking you've had some challenges recently. You were a pleasant fare, and I enjoyed getting to know you." Then, he added, "You have yourself a good day. And a good life."

"Thank you," she whispered, tears burning the backs of her

eyes. She was touched that a virtual stranger would be so generous. Maybe it was a sign that things were going to turn around for her.

She stood alone on an asphalt road in front of a gas station at the edge of Baker's Corner. She glanced around, not having any idea where she should go. As the town website had indicated, there were both *Englisch* and Amish folks milling about. Seeing some people dressed like she was, comforted her for she found herself more nervous than she'd predicted. She blew out her breath, praying that moving here wasn't a mistake. She picked up her suitcase and started walking—she needed to find a place to stay.

Thankfully, it didn't take long. Marlie found a quaint little inn not far from where she had been dropped off. Perhaps her driver had done that on purpose. Whatever the reason, she entered an attractive large home—complete with a wraparound porch and a white picket fence—called Pearl's Inn,

"How may I help you today?" an Amish man from behind a wooden counter asked her.

"I'd like a room." She swallowed her anxiety and laid a sum of money—a large portion of all she had—on the counter. "How long can I stay for this amount?"

The man tugged on his long, scraggly beard and then counted it out. He worked quickly, as if there was something more pressing to attend to.

"It'll get you room and board for a week. Maybe a day more," he replied. "Would you like to check in?"

"Yes," Marlie answered. That was almost all her money. She'd thought it would last much longer. A nervous tickle went down her spine.

He tucked her money into a money box and gave her a room key. "Your room is upstairs, right down the hallway, second on the left. You can't miss it. Will you be needing anything else?"

"No. I'm fine. Thank you."

As Marlie walked toward her room, she wondered how she would be able to support the child that was growing in her belly. Clearly, Grant would take no responsibility. Though Marlie wasn't showing yet, it had been the straw that broke the camel's back of her marriage, so to speak. Grant had never wanted children, and he didn't want to believe that he was the father of the child.

She supposed she could take him to court over it and prove he was, but she couldn't bear the thought of going to court again. She couldn't stomach the thought of strangers once again gawking at her and knowing her private business. Perhaps she was being foolish, but she couldn't help it. Their last time in she was in court had nearly killed her. Grant's lawyers had been ruthless, attacking everything she tried to utter, so much so, that she could barely get out a word.

Of course, a DNA sample would prove the child was Grant's.

But that thought made her shudder, too. It had to be her last resort. She would only do it if she found herself and her baby on the streets starving. Otherwise, no. She wanted no contact with Grant ever again.

Ever.

Marlie sighed, opening the door to her room. As she set her suitcase on the bed, she felt a sense of relief wash over her. Of peace, almost. There was no television in the room. No light switch. No plugs to recharge anything. There were no amenities that she had become accustomed to over the years. It was as if there was one goal in this place—simply to live life in the most basic of ways.

She inhaled, somehow knowing deep in her soul that she was in exactly the right place. She rubbed her stomach, praying it was so.

In a way, Marlie found it shocking that she was staying in an Amish inn. If she'd been told that even a week ago, she would have laughed. But, then, there were a lot of things in her life that she didn't recognize anymore. And this was certainly not how she thought she'd be living when expecting her first child.

Yet, here she was.

She started to unpack and found that there were just enough pegs on the wall for her hanging clothes. And of course, there was plenty of room in the heavy wooden dresser. She had no

Amish clothing, but she did have some clothes that were quite modest. She had brought long dresses with long sleeves – mostly three-quarter – and a pair of simple boots. That was similar to what she'd seen the Amish women wearing in photos online.

A knock at the door surprised her.

"One moment, please," Marlie called out. She walked to the door, wondering who would be coming to see her. She had no friends here, nor any acquaintances.

When she opened the door, an older Amish woman with a pleasant smile stood there.

"Hello, child, I'm Pearl Yoder."

Chapter Two

"I'm Marlie Jensen. It's nice to meet you," Marlie replied. "Did I forget to do something when I checked in?"

"*Ach, nee.* I just wanted to come and say hello. My husband and I run this inn," Pearl replied. "Ben said you had checked in for a week or so, and I wanted to see if there was anything I could do to help your stay go a little smoother."

"I-I'm not sure. Maybe. Is there a way I could get to know people around the area?" Marlie asked. "I-I came here to see what it's like to be Amish..."

"Did you now? May I come in?" Pearl's immediate interest made Marlie smile. She had a feeling she was going to like this woman.

"Sure..." Marlie opened the door a little wider as she spoke, and Pearl walked right in.

"I see you've already unpacked," Pearl said, looking at her clothes hanging on the pegs.

"I don't want to offend anyone," Marlie said. "I'm trying to dress conservatively so as not to stick out too much."

"These clothes are right pretty, but you'll stick out nevertheless," Pearl said, with a soft chuckle. Then, she continued, "But child, it ain't just Amish living here. We got *Englisch* folks, too, like you. But if you're concerned, I could ask a seamstress in our district if she'd make you a dress. They run about twenty dollars for the labor, if you got the money to spare."

"Uh... I don't think I can spare that much," Marlie confessed. "I barely had enough for the week here."

"I'm sorry to hear that." Pearl frowned a little as she spoke. "Then, don't worry about it. You just wear what you brought. It's fine anyway. And, if you're short of money, you could get a job."

"I didn't know where I could start looking for a job back in the city, let alone here in an Amish farming community." Marlie sighed. "I don't have many skills. It's been a ... rough few months."

"Well, get some rest, and I will be glad to help you figure it all out tomorrow—as best I can, anyway," Pearl said.

"Thank you."

With that, Pearl smiled again and left the room, the door shutting softly behind her.

Marlie kicked off her boots and lay down on the beautiful green and white quilt covering the bed, suddenly feeling beyond worn out.

When she had looked online, there had been no indication of job openings in Baker's Corner. But then, she probably hadn't been looking in the right place. She should check again.

Of course, there was no way she could get on the Internet at the inn. But she could use her phone instead of her computer. And then she remembered. She hadn't paid her latest bill and her service had been cut off. Grant had always taken care of such things for her in the past, but that was over.

She placed her hand on her stomach. Completely over.

Maybe if she got a job, she could reinstate her phone service. But that didn't solve anything for her right then. There was one upside, she supposed. No internet meant that she couldn't answer any possible emails from Grant about unfinished business between them.

That was a blessing. Besides, she dearly hoped there was no unfinished business between them. *Except the baby,* her mind insisted, but she shoved the thought away.

She took a deep breath. As she tried to slow her racing mind, that same earlier peace she'd felt before fell over her again. She had no idea why it came, or what it meant, but it was comforting. And right then, she needed anything that gave her comfort or hope.

"All right, Marlie," she whispered to herself. "You've got this. It may be a different kind of life here, but it's better than sticking around where Grant can hold anything over you."

With that, she closed her eyes. Her breathing slowed, and she fell into a restful sleep.

Marlie woke up to the smell of freshly baked bread. How could that be when she didn't have a suite, but just a room? As she roused, she realized that someone was rapping gently on her door.

"Come in," she called.

Pearl moved into her room and set some freshly baked bread on her dresser.

"I hope I didn't wake you, Marlie," Pearl spoke softly. "I'm glad to see you didn't lock the door. So many Englisch do. And I hope you don't mind me coming in again. I won't make a habit of it. But I just took this loaf out of the oven and buttered a few slices. I wanted you to have some while it's hot."

"Thank you," Marlie replied, sitting up and hanging her feet over the edge of the bed. "It smells heavenly."

Pearl laughed. "Do you want some now?"

Marlie nodded. Her stomach growled and she realized that she hadn't eaten for hours.

She took a piece of the thick bread Pearl offered her and took a big bite. It was heavenly, pure and simple. She immediately felt more energetic. She gazed at the kind woman before her and so many questions ran through her head. She cleared her throat.

"I want to learn everything I can while I'm here, if that's all right. Do you mind me asking why you don't use electricity and phones and such?"

Pearl smiled. "We believe that the best way to be close to *Gott* is to stay away from a lot of the modern conveniences. To be a people set apart. There are some communities that have embraced the barest of the modern conveniences, more than we do here in our district. Still, we do have phone shanties for business doings and such, just no phones in our homes. And we get by fine without electricity, you'll see." Pearl brought another slice of bread over. "In Baker's Corner, we use gas and propane for things. It runs our refrigerators and hot water heaters and such."

"I see..." Marlie pursed her lips. "So, what do you do if there is an emergency?"

"We hurry to a shanty and make a call to 911, just like you do."

"Is it possible ... I mean, can someone become Amish? If they weren't born Amish? Is that even possible?" Marlie asked. A trembling had started in her stomach, and she somehow felt that this could be one of the most important questions she had ever asked in her life.

"*Englischers*, as we call those that ain't Amish, sometimes think they can visit for a week and understand us," Pearl said. "But if someone is really serious about becoming Amish, then I reckon the best way is to live amongst us for a while first. And then, if they're still interested, take instruction from the bishop or one of the deacons. After that, if the person is approved, he or she can join church. It's a commitment, though. A lifelong commitment."

Marlie nodded, thinking about it.

"There's a lot of prejudice against the *Englischers* that stay with us in the inn."

"Why is that?" Marlie questioned.

"Because usually they don't want to learn of our way of life. They come to gawk at us," Pearl said hesitantly. "There are a lot of people that don't understand why we choose to live the way we do." She shrugged.

Marlie let it all sink in for a moment. She took another bite of bread, savoring the rich flavor and the melted butter. She couldn't begin to compare it with the store-bought bread she usually ate.

"Is your bread this good all the time?" She couldn't hide her pleasure, and Pearl chuckled.

"I would hope so. Is it better than what you're used to?"

"Yes, much better," Marlie said. "Not even in the same category. I love it. Is there any way I could get more of it?"

Pearl laughed outright at that. "Child, I'll teach you how to bake it yourself. Then, you can have it whenever you like."

"I would like that," Marlie answered. For some reason, tears sprang to her eyes at Pearl's offer, and she quickly brushed them away.

Pearl clearly noticed her tears, but despite the softening of her expression, she didn't mention them.

"I read that the Amish have accounts at the general store, kind of like in the olden days. Prairie days and such. And that you just pay up your account at the end of the month."

Pearl smiled. "My, but you have been reading up on us, haven't you? Well, it's true. Most of us have accounts at the mercantile. I tend to have money on hand, though," she went on. "A lot of people who stay here pay us in cash."

"Thanks for putting up with all my questions," Marlie said. "Do you have any questions for me while we're at it? Seems only fair."

"*Nee.* I just wanted to make sure you got some of my fresh bread. People from out of town do tend to love it." Pearl laughed. "Will you be all right by yourself for a while?"

"I should be, thank you. Actually, I think I'm going to go into town and see what I can find. Maybe I'll even see a *help wanted* sign," Marlie added. "Should I be aware of anything before I go?"

"Just be ready for lots of looks, Marlie," Pearl answered. "Strangers tend to be noticed."

Pearl patted Marlie's shoulder and left, and Marlie was alone in the room.

Lots of looks. Well, she would have to get used to that.

Chapter Three

Marlie slid the room key into her pocket and left the inn. She walked down the sidewalk that led further into town. Before long, she walked by a green sign boasting that she had arrived in Baker's Corner.

She smiled. It was time to see what life in the Amish community was really like.

As she walked down the street before coming to the main commerce area, she saw a few Amish people just off the road, milling about in the trees, picking fruit. It was a lovely scene, the grass and the trees with ladders leaning up against them. She even saw birds chasing each other through the sky. Many of the trees in the orchard seemed to be bearing a nice crop of fruit.

With a sudden surge of courage, she waved at a young Amish man who had glanced her way.

"Hello!" she called.

He smiled and nodded.

"What are you picking?" she hollered. She thought it might be cherries, although, they looked awfully big.

He came closer and stopped, still a good measure away. "Cherries. They don't usually grow well in these parts. We're lucky."

She returned his smile. "I love cherries."

"*Jah*, they seem to be popular with the *Englischers*. And I can understood why." The man chuckled. "Are you visiting?"

"I'm from the city," Marlie replied. "I'm hoping to stay a while."

Why she was divulging this information to a stranger, she couldn't say. But there was something about the young man—even though he was keeping his distance—that seemed kind. Maybe it was the expression on his face. Or the way he looked at her with such honest appraisal. She couldn't say.

"Another *Englischer* in our midst," he said and grinned. "And like all of them, you're mighty curious."

She smiled apologetically. "Yes. You could say that." She

realized that maybe her standing there talking to him would be considered odd. "Uh, my name is Marlie Jenkins."

"I'm Elijah." Elijah put down his bucket and said something to another couple of workers who were a few trees away. He turned back to her. "I'm good at answering questions. Been answering them all my life."

Marlie liked his forthright demeanor. "Have you lived here your entire life?"

After spending so long in only the company of Grant and his friends, Marlie had almost forgotten how to have a conversation that interested *her* at the most basic level. Outside of her recent conversation with Pearl, she was sorely out of practice.

"I was born here." He looked at her. "Last year, I was on my *rumspringa*. I went into the world, maybe even your city. Couldn't have been more different than my way life here, but I enjoyed it. So, I guess I did exactly what you're doing now. Investigating different ways of life." He ran his hand over his clean-shaven chin. "However, when it came time to return, I was right glad. I found the *Englisch* world lacking in something. *Jah,* you people have more gadgets and things, but..." Elijah paused and went on, "I missed my people terribly. Our simple way of life."

"What's *rumspringa*?" Marlie asked, attempting to pronounce the word correctly.

His ensuing explanation gave her all that she needed to understand why he had preferred his own community. Why, an Amish young person would have to feel completely misplaced when venturing out into the outside world—even if only for a short period of time before joining church.

As Elijah continued talking, she was shocked to learn that the Amish only attended school up through the eighth grade. Didn't they need more education than that? Didn't everyone?

But then, she had come upon Elijah picking cherries. She supposed farming didn't require regular schooling. Although, she was sure anyone majoring in agriculture would strongly disagree.

"What brings you here?" Elijah asked.

Marlie pursed her lips, unsure of exactly how to answer that question. She had to find something to say, though.

"I suppose it was time for a change in my life. I-I, well, I have just ended a relationship..." She sighed and her hands went instinctively to her stomach. He stared at her hands, and she felt sudden embarrassment. Did he suspect she was carrying a child?

But why should she care what he thought or didn't think about her?

He shuffled his foot in the dirt, clearly uncomfortable. Why in the world had she felt the need to blab out her business? She dropped her hands from her stomach and grew silent.

Elijah cleared his throat. "Baker's Corner is a rather small Amish district compared to some of the communities out in Pennsylvania. If you want to see big communities, *that's* where you should go."

"Oh?" Marlie questioned, her embarrassment forgotten. "I imagine there are quite a few Amish communities in Pennsylvania."

"*Jah*," Elijah answered and then he said some further words in a language she didn't understand.

"Pennsylvania Dutch, right? And I'm thinking that *jah* means yes?" Marlie asked with a smile, feeling increasingly comfortable with him.

Elijah nodded. "Sometimes I forget that *Englischers* don't speak our language. We speak a mixture of English and Pennsylvania Dutch. It's a derivative of Dutch, but that's about all I know of the history of the language." Elijah laughed.

The next fifteen minutes or so was spent in Elijah's company. He even pointed out his buggy parked beside some of the trees. He showed her how he lit the lamps on each side of his buggy at night to make driving safer. Other buggies, he told her, had fancier battery lights and some even had propane heaters inside.

"Well, I've been jawing long enough. I need to get back at it. The others are going to want my help again with the picking, and I've abandoned them for far too long. I don't imagine some of them are any too pleased with me as it is," Elijah said, excusing himself.

"Will you be in trouble?"

He grinned at her. "*Nee*. They half expect it. Remember, I just got back from *rumspringa* and haven't joined church yet. They know I'm still at ease talking with *Englischers*."

"Thank you for all the information, Elijah. I'm sure I'll see you around," Marlie said.

"All right then. Have a good day, Marlie," Elijah bade her farewell. She waved at him as he left her to get back to the trees. She was awfully grateful to have learned more things about the Amish and their way of life. Elijah had been more helpful than he might have guessed.

She turned away, continuing toward town. Now that she was alone, she wanted to explore the town center. She found that it was small and pleasant, quite tidy and clean, actually. However, there were no help wanted signs to be seen anywhere.

There was a good-sized general goods shop, which sold all manner of things for daily life. She walked through it, noting that there were brands she was familiar with and many that she wasn't. She also noticed that most of the merchants in town had oversized parking lots with hitching posts in them. She smiled at the sight.

She passed a seamstress shop and a doctor's office. She took special note of the doctor's office, knowing that she would need to make an appointment there soon. She had no health insurance anymore, so she hoped the fee wouldn't be too steep. But she couldn't put if off forever. Pregnant women needed to be checked regularly.

The most surprising shop Marlie found was probably a small jam and jelly store. It sold jams, jellies, honey, and other homemade goodies. Someday, she hoped to sample them all.

Chapter Four

After Marlie explored the community center to her heart's content, she couldn't shake the vision of the jams in the little specialty shop. However, she didn't have the money to spend on such things. So, with exaggerated disappointment, she walked back toward the inn. There was a slight sag to her step, and she scolded herself soundly for being so petty.

But, oh, the cherry jam had smelled delicious – made with freshly picked cherries that had been sold just for that purpose, or so she was informed by the sweet shopkeeper.

She returned to the inn, deciding she would love to go talk to Pearl Yoder again. When she looked in the lobby, Pearl was not to be found. She rang the bell at the front desk.

The bell was answered by Ben Yoder.

"May I help you?" His voice was gruff and he seemed preoccupied. Marlie wondered if he thought of his business at the inn as a bother.

"I'm looking for Pearl... Is she around?" Marlie asked.

"You just missed her," Ben replied, rubbing his hands together with a rough scraping sound. "I'll make sure she comes to your room when she gets back." With that, he nodded and was gone before she could even respond.

Marlie got the distinct feeling that Mr. Yoder didn't like her much, though she could think of no reason why he shouldn't. It couldn't be because she was single and pregnant—for that he didn't even know. And she wasn't showing yet; her stomach was still mostly flat. If she hadn't gotten confirmation before the divorce had been finalized, *she* wouldn't have believed she was pregnant.

Regardless, she decided that she didn't need to be worried about Ben's response to her. At least, not right then.

Marlie walked to her room. As she opened the door, she remembered that she hadn't finished the bread from that morning. She smiled a little. Snatching up the plate, she sat down on the quilt. The bread may have been better with those cherry preserves, but still, with just the butter alone it was fine with her.

This time, the bread was cold, but she found that it was still as heavenly as it had been that morning. She took another bite, savoring the taste.

The rest of the day passed slowly. Marlie wasn't sure if she should be doing something specific to find a job. Since she hadn't noticed any help wanted signs in any of the shops downtown, what else might there be for her?

She went downstairs and spent the rest of the afternoon in the lobby. There was no use in sitting in her room all day alone. She rested in one of the large chairs off to the right of a cast iron stove. The spot was out of the way, but it kept her within sight of the door. She did want to be able to catch Pearl as soon as she came in.

"I thought you were going to stay in your room for the rest of the day," Ben Yoder's voice echoed in the lobby.

"Oh, I hope I'm not bothering you," she said quickly. "It's just that what I need to discuss with Pearl is important. If I sit here, I can see her as soon as she comes in."

"I told you I'd tell her. Once she's here, you can talk to her, as I said before." He snorted and walked away, leaving her more confused than ever about his attitude toward her. She found herself quite grateful that he'd left her alone again.

Not long after that, Pearl showed up.

"Marlie! I didn't think you would have returned so soon from exploring the community," Pearl exclaimed upon seeing her. "I heard from young Elijah that he gave you an education of sorts."

Marlie nodded. "He did. It was real nice of him, and helpful, too. Uh... I would like to talk to you... Do you have a moment to spare?"

"I have time, *jah*," Pearl said. "Would you like to speak in your room, or did you have somewhere else in mind?"

"My room works fine," Marlie said.

"You go on up. I'll make us some tea and be right with you."

Marlie went to her room and waited on her bed for Pearl.

About ten minutes later, Pearl came in smiling with a tray. Two steaming cups of tea sat on the tray. Pearl handed her one, and she took the other.

"Now, what did you want to talk to me about, child?"

"I have to confess that I'm feeling a bit frantic. I didn't see any help needed signs in town." She paused and circled the warm cup of tea with her hands, letting its welcome heat sink into her. "You mentioned about me getting a job earlier, and I do need one."

Pearl reached over and touched her elbow. "We can ask around," she said. "There's not too much rush, is there?"

Marlie took a deep breath. "There is, kind of. I need a job while I'm here, and I don't think there are many things I could easily do. I don't have many skills. To be honest, I haven't worked many jobs in my life. Well, hardly any in fact. And there's something else. I ... well, I'm almost three months pregnant."

She held her breath, waiting for Pearl's response.

Pearl's lips parted, and she put her cup of tea back down on the tray. "Why, Marlie. That's right lovely. *Bopplis* are a blessing from the Lord *Gott*."

Marlie bit her lip to keep from crying.

"And the *boppli*'s *dat*?" Pearl asked.

"He, uh, he's not in the picture. He doesn't even want the child. We're divorced."

Pearl gasped. "*Ach!* I never heard such a thing. Not to want your own *boppli*...?" She paused. "I'm so sorry, child. What shall you do?"

"I'm going to raise the baby myself," Marlie declared, feeling a stirring of determination.

Pearl nodded. "Of course, you are. Of course. Why, what else would you do?"

"It's going to be all right," Marlie went on, with more courage than she felt. "But still... I need a job. I mean, women raise children by themselves all the time. I can do this. But I have to have money."

Pearl tilted her head. "In our community, women don't raise children by themselves much at all. *Ach,* Marlie. I'm so sorry. This will be hard for you."

Marlie gathered all her courage for what she was about to ask. "Is there anyway I could have a job here in the inn? I mean, is there anything that you need help with? I'm good at housework. I am. And I'll work hard. You'd be happy you hired me. Really, you would. I'd do a good job." Marlie stopped abruptly, realizing she'd turned to begging. She sucked in her breath, suddenly ashamed to be putting Pearl in such a position.

Pearl gave her a tender look, and Marlie blinked back her tears.

"I'm sorry," Marlie said. "Forget I asked. It was rude of me. I don't know what I was thinking."

"*Nee.* I wasn't rude," Pearl said, her voice soft. "I'll see what I can do. However, I must warn you that my husband will not likely be very excited about hiring an *Englischer*."

Marlie shook her head. "Please. Don't make any trouble on account of me. I'm sure something else will work out. Yes. Of course, it will. Pretend I didn't even ask."

Pearl had been so kind to her already, and Marlie didn't want to put her in an awkward position with her husband.

Marlie had already seen first-hand how crochety the man could be.

Pearl's eyes narrowed and she stared off into space. "Now, don't you fret, child. Hmm. I'm not getting any younger. Some help might do me quite a lot of good. There's so much cleaning to be done. I will see what I can do. I make no promises, mind, but I'll see what I can do."

"Anything that's possible would be *wunderbaar*, as you say," Marlie replied with a hopeful smile. "I believe that's the word you use for wonderful here."

"You catch on right quick, child. That will be helpful for getting along in the community. If you keep that up, you might learn Pennsylvania Dutch faster than any *Englischer* I've seen." Pearl stood and took Marlie's near-empty cup. "I'll be going, then."

"All right. Thank you, Pearl. Truly," Marlie murmured.

Marlie shook her boots off and placed them on the rag rug next to her bed. She lay back on the quilt and stared at the ceiling. Her feet hurt from her excursion into town. She wriggled her toes, trying to ease their discomfort.

For the hundredth time, she was grateful that she hadn't experienced any morning sickness with this pregnancy. She wasn't sure how she'd be able to cope with that on top of everything else.

She closed her eyes, and Grant's face floated in front of her mind. She quickly sat back up. She didn't want to think of him. She shivered at the mere thought of him. She rubbed her eyes. How long would it be before she could remember him without feeling heartsick? Without feeling resentment? Without feeling like she'd been a huge fool for getting involved with him in the first place?

"Ah, little one," she whispered to her stomach. "I'm so sorry. I'm so sorry that you won't have a dad. I should have chosen better. Much better. It's all my fault. Please forgive me."

And then, she placed her hands over her belly and imagined what her child might look like.

Chapter Five

The week slowly came around. Marlie heard nothing from Pearl about a possible job, and she didn't want to ask again. She'd already been pushy enough with the kind woman. So, she spent her days walking around the community, trying to orient herself to the way of life in Baker's Corner.

At the Inn, she avoided Ben as much as possible. Although, she did run into him from time to time, which was to be expected. After all, she took her meals there, even though she sometimes ate at different times than he did. Still, he was around. She put on her best behavior in front of him, despite his sourness. She had to wonder if he was sour to everyone, or was it just to her? Other guests came and went regularly, and in truth, he didn't seem overly friendly with any of them.

When she was feeling rested, watching Ben was actually amusing. Whoever heard of such a grouch being in the hospitality business?

One time, he implied that she should go back to her husband, which could only mean that Pearl had indeed told him about her pregnancy. Well, she figured he'd have to know soon enough, especially if she was able to work there. But that possibility seemed to move further and further from view.

The second to the last day before her room and board ran out, she found Pearl sitting in the chair in the hallway outside her room. She stood up as Marlie approached.

"I have news for you, Marlie," Pearl stated. "Would you be willing to discuss this in your room?"

"Yes. Yes, of course," Marlie replied, her voice shaking. She was afraid Pearl was going to tell her no, and she didn't want to hear it. She'd found no other work, and she had no idea what she was going to do next—how she was going to take care of herself and a baby. She had no one. No one at all.

Grant had been right. She had no friends, and her family had disowned her years before. Her family couldn't stand Grant, and when Marlie defied them by marrying him, they had thrown her out of the family. How Marlie wished she would have listened to them. It would have saved her such heartache. But it was too late now. There was no going back.

Pearl led her into the room, and Marlie sat down on the bed. "What do you want to tell me?"

Pearl smiled at her and the wrinkles around her eyes deepened with obvious joy.

"I've convinced Ben that we need extra help around the inn," she said. "I would like you to fill that gap. So, dear child, would you be interested in earning your room and board, as well as a little extra on the side?"

Marlie jumped off the bed. "Do you mean it? I mean, really mean it?"

Pearl chuckled at her enthusiasm. "I mean it, child."

"You're not teasing me?"

"*Ach*, why would I do such a thing?"

Marlie stepped close to Pearl and threw her arms around her. "I would love it. *Denke*, Pearl, *denke!*"

Marlie could hardly believe it was happening. How had Pearl gotten Ben to listen and agree? It was beyond wonderful. Marlie let go of Pearl and simply stood before her, grinning.

"*Gut*," Pearl added. "Then you will start after your rent runs out. To begin with, you will only be earning three dollars extra per week, as that's all we can afford in addition to room and board."

"That's better than I could have asked for. And now I can save some money for the future. And maybe even to buy a dress that really fits in here. I'd like that a lot."

"I appreciate your heart," Pearl said. "There ain't nothing stopping you from dressing Amish. Just know that there's a whole lot more to being Amish than putting on a dress and *kapp*."

"I know, Pearl. I, well, I like it here. I like being with you. I want to learn more."

"And learn more, you shall. We can check into a dress, but I don't want you to get ahead of yourself."

Marlie nodded.

"How are you feeling?"

"I'm feeling fine. I'm not really showing yet, am I?"

"*Nee*, child. We'll have to take your condition into consideration for your dress. Get one made that can be let out as time goes on."

"Yes. I mean, *jah*."

"You can go to the seamstress today and ask, if you like. She'll be closed tomorrow because it's Sunday. We have a visiting day this week. Church service is next week," Pearl elaborated. "Now, the seamstress will be open for another hour and a half or so. It only takes twenty minutes to walk there from here."

"I'll be going then," Marlie said, unable to contain her

excitement. "Again, *denke*, for all that you've done for me. I'm so grateful."

"You're welcome, Marlie."

Pearl walked with her toward the front door of the inn. It was odd—in Marlie's mind, Pearl was becoming the grandmother Marlie had never had. Marlie would never say so out loud, of course, She wouldn't want to overstep. But still, Pearl had become that dear to her.

Marlie left the inn and started down the sidewalk toward town. Though the Inn was technically part of Baker's Corner, it wasn't within the town limits. Ben had informed her of that just the other day. But the inn was close enough that it felt part of the community to Marlie. She pressed her hands to her stomach. She was feeling more and more a part of the community herself. She could hardly believe that she would get to stay. Of all the places in Indiana she could have chosen to move to, this had to be the best place by far.

Turning a corner on her way to the seamstress's shop, she bumped smack into an Amish man about her age.

"Oh, I'm sorry," she apologized, regaining her balance.

The man nodded, smiled absently at her, before continuing on his way. She was still feeling so cheerful about her job right then that she wished he would have paused long enough for her to introduce herself. But he appeared to be in quite a hurry, or perhaps he wasn't inclined to stop and chat with an *Englischer*.

The seamstress shop was small and cozy, with two rooms. There was one room to seat customers who were waiting to give their orders. It was decorated with samples and bolts of fabric and also there were heavy books of dress patterns scattered about. There was another room she couldn't see into. It was probably where they took measurements and made sure the clothing fit right when the order was complete.

"Are you visiting the community?" a young woman greeted her from the counter. The woman wasn't Amish, but she was dressed very conservatively. "I don't think I've seen you around here before."

"*Jah*, I was visiting. But now, I'll be staying. I'm interested in ordering a dress."

"I see. Why don't you come back and get measured, and then we can talk more about it?" The woman gestured toward the second room.

"*Denke*. I'm Marlie Jensen, by the way."

The young woman nodded and took her through to the other room in the shop.

"I'm Rose. All right then, Marlie. Step up onto that platform for me," Rose instructed. Marlie did as she was asked, and then stood very still while she was measured.

Rose was quiet while she worked, her brow furrowed in concentration. The only words exchanged were instructions. Marlie was told to raise her arms, to lower them, to stand still, not to suck her belly in.

"All right. I have your measurement. What style were you thinking?"

"I'd like the dress to be Amish style. But it will have to be let out at the waist real soon. I'll need a lot more stomach room in the next six months."

Rose raised her brow. "I see. We can accommodate that."

Marlie could tell that Rose wanted to ask her questions about the style she had chosen and about the maternity aspect of the dress, but she was too professional to do so.

"It will take about a week to get your dress made. You can look through the samples of fabric in the other room. Considering your choice of style, you'll want to look through the solid and subdued colors."

"Is it possible to pay on time?" Marlie asked.

"You mean in installments?"

"Yes. *Jah*."

"I can do that if you pay fifty percent up front."

To do that, Marlie would have to take an advance on her pay, which she was loathe to do. "I'll need to see the final cost."

Rose opened the door and motioned Marlie to follow her back to the original room..

Marlie was given the cost, and of course, it was well above what she would earn in a week, let alone two. It'd probably be closer to two months before she could get that kind of money together.

"So. You're interested in paying half of that today and placing the order?" Rose asked.

Marlie shook her head. "I wouldn't be able to pay even half right now, but *denke* for giving me a figure to work with. Is there no way I could pay less?"

"For an Amish dress, that is the price. I'm sorry if it doesn't work for you." Rose studied her for a minute. "If you want to, you can talk to my boss when she returns in ten minutes or so."

"Oh, that's not necessary. I'll come around again when I can afford something," Marlie said. "Have a good day. And *denke* for your help. It was nice to meet you."

"You too, Marlie." Rose pursed her lips. "And Marlie, most Amish make their own clothes. Maybe you can find someone to help you. Or maybe, you could sew the dress yourself."

Marlie shook her head and nearly laughed at the vision of herself able to sew a full dress. There was no way she could possibly do that on her own. "I appreciate the advice, Rose.

Denke," she said again and the bell above the door tinkled on her way out.

The walk back to the inn was quiet and uneventful. Marlie was discouraged that it would take months to get the money she needed for the seamstress. Factoring in the other things she'd have to buy, it would take much longer than she'd hoped to purchase an Amish dress.

Perhaps she could trade in one of her old dresses and get an Amish dress in return? She could sell one of her old dresses to an *Englischer* if she really wanted to. Couldn't she? Although looking about the town, she didn't see any sign of a consignment shop.

Marlie was so consumed with her thoughts that she bumped into someone again – this time right outside the door to the inn. Her face flamed hot at being so careless twice in the same afternoon.

"Oops. I'm sorry," Marlie apologized. She looked up to see that it was the same man she had run into earlier. Her mouth opened in complete embarrassment. "Oh, no! I'm so sorry. You must think me a total klutz. I feel ridiculous."

"*Ach*, it's all right." The man smiled with amusement. "I imagine we could turn this around and say that I'm the one that bumped into you. So I s'pose I should know your name. I mean, we've run into each other twice now."

Marlie laughed despite herself. "Marlie. Marlie Jensen."

"I'm Abel Yoder," he told her. He smiled again then, and she was drawn to his simple warmth and clear blue eyes.

"Yoder? Then are you related to Pearl and Ben Yoder?" Marlie asked.

"I'm Ben's cousin," he replied. "I usually work at the factory, but work gets slow around this time of year."

"I see," she added. "So, what do you do when work is slow?"

"I'm around here a lot. I help Ben in his barn. He's got some major repairs that need seeing to," Abel answered. "Are you new around here?"

"I was visiting from the city," Marlie replied. "But I'll be staying for a while now."

He smiled, showing his even white teeth. "That's nice. You'll like Baker's Corner. But I need to be going. Perhaps, I'll see you around."

"*Jah*. I'm staying here at the inn," she added, pointing to the door just behind him.

"Then I'll surely see you around," he said.

Marlie went inside and went up to her room. Abel Yoder seemed nice. She chuckled. She couldn't imagine running into the same person twice—and on the same day. What were the odds?

She rubbed her arm where they'd collided the last time. There had been something undeniable when she bumped into him the second time. Almost as if she was destined to meet him. Her smile faded as she realized what she was thinking. No. No. No. She couldn't entertain any such thoughts. Goodness, but what was the matter with her?

Hadn't she learned her lesson as far as men were concerned?

Chapter Six

Two days later, Marlie officially started her job at the inn. She began with cleaning the bedrooms, to see how she could handle it. Marlie was so delighted to be working for Pearl that she would have gladly started with scrubbing the toilets. Which of course, would likely be her next assignment.

Two of the bedrooms were side-by-side, and they had been vacated the night before. Ben was expecting guests to fill their places later that day, so getting those two rooms clean and ready was a top priority for her. If she could get onto Ben's good side by doing an especially thorough job, it might go better between them. Marlie was aware that he wasn't pleased about her pregnancy, either. And she dreaded growing bigger and more obvious. So, if she could make some headway with him before then, all the better.

Before the noon meal, both of the rooms were spotlessly clean. Marlie was a little out of breath, which dismayed her. She couldn't be losing her energy so easily; that wouldn't do. Yet she had been going up and down the stairs all morning. And she'd been down in the basement, too, to do the laundry. Pearl had told her that most Amish folks did laundry only on Mondays, but that didn't really work when one owned an inn.

It had taken a while for Marlie to get the hang of the wringer washer machine, but once she did, she found it surprisingly efficient. Ben had strung the basement with clothesline for the winter. But since the day was sunny, she hung the sheets and towels out in the yard.

On her way to the kitchen to help Pearl with the noon meal, Ben stopped her.

"Good morning, Mr. Yoder," she said politely.

"You done with them rooms?" He didn't mince words.

"Yes. I mean, *jah*. They're ready."

"And you was thorough? And you felt all right?" He gave her a grudging look. "Being... uh, being ... in the family way?"

"Yes. *Jah*."

"What about your husband?" he asked, his voice now taking a condemning tone. "You ought to go back to him. It ain't right for a young woman to leave her husband, especially when she is ... in the family way."

Marlie did not want to talk about Grant right then. She hadn't thought of him the entire morning, which had been a real accomplishment. But now, she had no choice. There he was again—hovering over her. Would she never be rid of him?

"I can't go back to my husband. He left me," she told Ben the truth. "It's over. Splitting up wasn't my idea. I came here hoping to find a little peace and maybe healing."

She watched Ben's face while she spoke, and she noticed the tension around his mouth lessening. Was he softening toward her?

She drew in a deep breath. "I've found the beginnings of peace here. I can't say why, exactly, but I have. And I want to thank both you and Pearl for it." She bit the corner of her lip, waiting for his reaction.

"He left you?" he asked, his voice still harsh. "*Englisch* men is fools. Plain and simple." He pulled on his beard. "I s'pose I ought to leave you to your work now."

Well, he wasn't exactly exuding warmth, but at least he hadn't kept scolding her. She'd take it as progress.

"*Denke*," she said softly.

He grunted and turned away, and Marlie went into the kitchen to find Pearl.

"Ah, there you are," Pearl said to her before she had a chance to speak. "Come on, then. We're going to fall behind if you don't get at those potatoes."

"Right away," Marlie said and went to work on the potatoes. "Ben stopped me on my way to ask if I was truly pregnant and to tell me to go back to my husband."

Pearl sighed. "That don't surprise me at all. He never did understand the whole idea of divorce." Pearl watched her peeling the potato. "Have you ever made mashed potatoes?"

"A few times. They were my mother's favorite thing to make for Thanksgiving," Marlie explained. "I know what to do, Pearl."

"All right," Pearl said and let her be.

As Marlie peeled one potato after another, she relaxed into the rhythm of the work. Her mind wandered to her run-in with Abel the other day. She hadn't seen him since then, but she knew there would be plenty of time in his company if he would be helping Ben. For some reason, the thought excited her.

Then, she remembered something she had learned the other day. Amish men never married someone outside of their faith. She gulped and her hand with the peeler stopped moving. *Married?* What was she thinking?

She needed to rein in her thoughts.

She started peeling again, but her mind refused to budge from her thoughts of Abel. She'd mentioned to Pearl that she was interested in possibly becoming Amish, but was she really? And she didn't have only herself to consider anymore. She was carrying a child. A dear, innocent child. Whatever decisions she made needed to be weighed with that in mind.

In truth, the child's needs must be considered ahead of her own, and she was fine with that. She smiled down at her stomach, relieved that the baby was becoming something precious to her. Things had become so disturbing around the time she'd learned of her pregnancy, she'd had no time to really, truly consider it. No time to revel in the beauty and magnificence of carrying a child.

But now? The baby was becoming more and more real to her every day. The week before, she'd gone to the doctor. She'd been surprised at being able to get an appointment so easily. The receptionist had been able to squeeze her in that very day.

During her appointment, Marlie had heard the baby's heartbeat, and it had filled her with such amazement and joy that she was sure she'd stopped breathing—at least for a moment or two.

"Pearl, what can you tell me about Abel?" she blurted out without preamble. She felt her face grow warm with embarrassment. What would Pearl think of her to be asking such a question? But Pearl took it in stride.

"Well, he's Ben's cousin for starters," she began. "He works at the factory most of the time. He was temporarily laid off since there's not much work to be done right now. When he's here, he's either helping Ben fix up the old barn behind the inn, or he's caring for our animals."

Marlie finished peeling the last potato and started to cut the potatoes into chunks.

Pearl grinned. "That boy will work with anything we happen to have on the farm at the moment. He favors our few cows, but he cares for the pigs, too. To be honest, it's a big help to Ben. The constant repairs around the inn keep Ben busy enough."

She wiped her brow and went on. "We're thinking about selling some of the pigs off. Could raise a tidy sum of money."

Marlie laughed. "We *Englischers*, myself included, love our bacon."

"As do we. Why do you ask about Abel?"

"I ran into him a couple of days ago, and I was curious. That's all," Marlie answered.

"I find it mighty strange that Abel also asked about you. He wanted to know how long you'd been staying at the inn, and what you intended to do here. I think he wanted to know if you plan to stay permanent-like," Pearl speculated. "I can't imagine why, nor why he wanted to ask me. Seemed downright nosy." She laughed.

Marlie bit back her smile of pleasure. Abel must have felt it, too—that fluttery feeling when they touched because of her clumsiness. The knowledge made Marlie's pulse increase.

As much as she didn't want to admit it, she was interested in Abel Yoder. She certainly wasn't ready to have her heart broken again, especially so soon after Grant. But there was something about Abel that drew her in. And she trusted him. She gave a start at the realization. How could she trust someone she'd barely even met? Besides, could she trust her *own* judgment? Hadn't she trusted Grant at one time, too?

She set the potatoes on the stove to boil.

"Is there anything I can do to help while the potatoes cook?" Marlie asked.

"If you want to make some lemonade, that'd be fine with me," Pearl answered. "The lemons are sitting on the shelf right above the counter there." She pointed vaguely in the direction of the shelves.

Marlie had never made lemonade from scratch before, but it didn't prove to be hard. She juiced the lemons and made sure she added sufficient sugar to the water. When she was done with that and put the pitcher in the refrigerator to chill, she checked on the potatoes. They weren't soft enough yet; however, they were getting there.

Pearl kept her busy as she waited for the potatoes to finish. After the lemonade, it was time to make a gravy for the potatoes. Pearl had already drained the juices from the meat; it was just a matter of thickening it and adding some spices. Marlie was on stir duty. Every now and then, she reached over to stick a fork through a potato boiling beside the gravy.

The noon meal was ready after about an hour's labor from her, and probably double that from Pearl. It smelled amazing and when everyone, including the guests, sat down to eat, no one was disappointed.

"Thank you for your help with the dishes," Pearl announced when the kitchen was *red* up. "You did well this morning, Marlie. And you're finished with the rooms we asked you to clean earlier?"

"*Jah*," Marlie answered. "I finished them before Ben stopped me in the hallway earlier."

"*Gut*," Pearl observed. "Well, we have three more rooms to be cleaned. If you'll give me a few minutes, I'll get you the room numbers, and you can clean them as well."

"That'd be *gut*," Marlie replied. She did her best to use the Amish words she had been learning instead of their English counterparts. She was eager to learn as many words as she could and dreamed of the day when she might be able to hold a simple conversation in Pennsylvania Dutch.

"I'm still impressed that you're eager to use some of our

words almost as if you'd grown up here," Pearl told her with a smile. "If you really have interest in joining us—joining church, it'll serve you well to know our language."

Chapter Seven

Once Marlie had the numbers for the other rooms she would be cleaning, she got right to it. As she did so, she was delighted to again run into Abel—although this time, not literally.

"This is becoming a habit, Marlie," Abel teased, looking pleased to see her. "How are you doing?"

"I'm doing fine," she replied. "What about you?"

"I think I have bruises from where you ran into me the last two times." He laughed.

At first, she thought he might be making fun of her, but listening to his laughter, she could tell he was simply joking.

"At least this time, I saw you before crashing into you," she responded. "So, that's progress, right?"

"It is," he said, stepping aside. She smiled and continued on her way, trying to suppress a blush that felt hot on her cheeks. My, but he affected her. She supposed it would be wise to avoid him whenever possible, but she didn't think she could.

Seeing him brightened her day, and she was hungry for anything that made her days more pleasant.

She arrived at the first room. It wasn't too bad, and she knew it wouldn't take long. Cleaning the rooms helped her feel productive and useful. But as she scrubbed, her mind kept going back to Abel. She fought her thoughts, focusing hard on dusting and sweeping, but it was no good. She kept visualizing Abel's warm smile and the twinkle in his eyes.

You're an Englischer, she told herself. *He won't look at you twice.*

When she was nearly finished with the room, she ran downstairs to grab some window cleaner. Pearl hadn't asked her to clean the windows, but she had noted more than one smear on the glass.

Abel was going down the stairs in front of her. When he noticed her, he paused.

"Hi again, Marlie."

She forced herself to breathe evenly.

"Ben tells me that you have been here for over a week. How do you like Baker's Corner so far?"

"I like it," she answered frankly. "I... Well, I needed a new beginning and it seems I've found it." She glanced down at the heavy wooden handrail. "It's peaceful here. I like that."

He nodded. "I imagine it isn't my business, but I was curious. Hope you don't mind me asking. I'm glad you're finding what you're looking for here."

She considered his words. "Me, too. I can't imagine growing up in such a place." Her mind went to her unborn child. "It seems like the perfect place to raise children."

"I s'pose it is," he said. He shifted his weight from one foot to the other. "Well, I'll let you get on with your work."

"I'm just going down to get some window cleaner," she told him. "I want to be quick about my work today. I don't think Ben would appreciate it if I stalled longer than I need to. They want these rooms clean as soon as possible."

"When you're done, would you like to accompany me to dinner?" he asked. "You know, so you can get to know Baker's Corner a bit better."

Her eyes widened. She hadn't expected this. Was he supposed to be seen in public with an *Englisch* girl? She didn't think so. She glanced down at her clothes. She still hadn't gotten an Amish dress or head covering, so even though she was dressed a bit old-fashioned, there would be no mistaking her for Amish.

He looked uncomfortable, and she realized she was taking too long to answer.

"So, you're thinking of eating elsewhere? Not here?" she asked.

"I was thinking of treating you to dinner at the little diner on the edge of town. Would you like that?"

"I would like that. *Denke* for inviting me," Marlie said, wondering if there was any way she could get Amish clothes in the next couple hours. Impossible, she knew.

"*Gut.* I was thinking that we might as well get to know each other since you're living with my kin."

"*Jah*," she replied. "So, where should I meet you?"

"How about we meet at the front door of the inn? About five o'clock?"

She nodded. "Sounds fine. I'll see you at five, then."

"See you," he said and walked away.

Marlie's heart was fluttering out of control. An evening with Abel? How had she gotten so lucky? Never, never would she have guessed it could ever happen. She still wondered at it. She wasn't sure how she'd be able to concentrate on her work the rest of the afternoon.

She continued on to the kitchen and found some glass cleaner beneath the sink. She grabbed it and went back upstairs. Despite her excitement, the repetitive nature of the cleaning helped her feel as though she had gained some kind of control over her life again. For so long, she had felt under Grant's control. But no longer.

She was making her own decisions now. Meeting new people. *Wonderful* new people.

She flew through the rest of the rooms, keeping an eye on her watch. Though there were clocks in the main rooms of the inn, there were no clocks in the bedrooms. She wanted to have enough time to freshen up before dinner.

When it was twenty minutes to five, she finished her work. She dashed to her room and changed her clothing to another conservative outfit. Then she brushed through her long hair again, twisting it into a bun at the nape of her neck, like Pearl did.

She went downstairs to the front door. Abel met her at five on the dot.

"I hope you haven't been waiting," he mused when he saw her already there. "Are you always so punctual?"

"Usually. I was just glad that I finished everything in time," she replied. "Should we go?"

"Let's," he responded.

They walked out the front door of the inn into the warm air, and she wondered what would happen on this outing. She was sure it wasn't officially a date—it couldn't be, but she wondered what would happen nevertheless.

She managed to shake her thoughts of possible romance away. They walked in pleasant silence, matching their strides with an easy gait. Every now and again, she glanced at Abel from the corner of her eye. His face was relaxed into a half smile, and she found herself smiling in return even though he wasn't looking at her.

They arrived at the quaint diner, and he opened the door for her.

"*Denke*, Abel."

He nodded, and then walked in after her. They were seated at a small table. He sat across from her, and she was suddenly tongue-tied. Plus, their presence was being noted by others in the diner, and that only made her feel more self-conscious.

"So, how long have you been interested in our Amish way of life?" Abel started the conversation.

"For an awful long time. When I was a lot younger, I read books on the Amish, and I was fascinated. I was enchanted by life on the farm and the lanterns and the horses and the buggies. But it was only when I came here that I was able to actually act on that interest," she said wistfully. "I think there was something in the stars that made me move here."

"Or *Gott's* will," Abel said, looking intently into her eyes.

"*Jah*," she murmured. "Or God's will."

"So, you're glad you came?" he asked, and she nodded. "That's *gut*. So, you might, uh, you might want to stay here forever?"

She laughed, suddenly uncomfortable with such probing questions. She wondered if Abel knew about the baby. Had Ben told him? She had no idea, nor did she want to bring it up right then.

"Do I want to stay forever?" she repeated thoughtfully. "I haven't spent enough time here to make that decision, but it is possible. Were you born here?"

"I was born here. But I transferred my church membership to another small community about an hour's drive away, where I work. Ben wants me to come back here to live, and in truth, I'd like to. Maybe I should come and help Ben at the inn full-time. But anyway, as it stands now, I come back every chance I get," he said. "What does your family think of your decision to live here?"

"My family doesn't know where I am. I was cut off from them a while ago, and so we don't talk."

"I'm sorry," he said, looking both surprised and sympathetic. "Do you plan to reconnect with them if you don't stay here?"

"I might look for them either way," she answered, wanting to change the subject. "So. How long have you been working in a factory?"

"For about five years now. It's a rather boring kind of work. We build recreational trailers and the finished products are really quite amazing," he said. "I enjoy the work okay, I suppose, when it's not too slow. But really, I prefer to work the land. Or work with animals."

The conversation continued, and they talked about different Amish ways and customs, and she told him about her customs. More than once, they marveled at the differences, and more than once, they ended up laughing. Marlie found that she was enjoying herself thoroughly, even though they continued to be stared at. Once, during the main course, Abel leaned close and whispered, "Don't worry about folks gawking. I'm used to it from *Englischers* passing through, but even I have to admit that my own kind are staring this time."

"It's because of my clothes, isn't it?"

"It's because you're not Amish," he said, confirming her thoughts. "But it's all right. Don't ask me how I know it is. I just know."

Chapter Eight

Over the weeks, Marlie found herself becoming closer and closer to Pearl. The older Amish woman talked non-stop to her as they worked on the noon meal or supper together. She would talk about all sorts of things – her growing up years and her disappointment at not having any children of her own. Marlie asked questions from time to time, and she even asked Pearl for mini-language lessons as they worked. Marlie found everything Pearl shared fascinating. As she learned more about Pearl and about the beliefs in the district, she found that there was an increased yearning in her heart.

That didn't stop her from feelings of confusion at times, though. Her pregnancy was showing now, even though she tried to make it as inconspicuous as possible. But it didn't help that even the loosest dress she had was too fitted and didn't leave much room for the bump.

She would need new dresses – regardless of whether she could pay for them or not. She needed true maternity dresses and she wanted them to be Amish. Marlie wondered if perhaps, Pearl would be willing to help her find a way to get maternity clothing, but she was hesitant to broach the subject.

Then, of course, there was Abel. He was around every day and had become someone she saw often. More than once, she'd promised herself to ignore him, but she never could. He was kind and funny and always had a moment to chat with her.

Of course, he had to be aware of her pregnancy now, though neither of them ever mentioned it. But the fact that he still spoke to her and teased her could only mean that Pearl or Ben had explained everything to him, and he was all right with it.

Marlie sometimes wondered if the other people in the community were judging Abel for being with her—the expectant *Englisch* woman. She'd worried about that constantly after their dinner at the local diner. Since then, he'd taken her in the buggy a time or two to get supplies at the mercantile. Each time, she felt people staring at them with disapproving eyes.

But they weren't dating or courting … at least, not officially. She was certain of it. For they couldn't be, could they? Not with the differences hanging between them.

"Marlie!" Pearl called up the stairs for her, pulling her from her thoughts. She took in a deep breath and left the room she'd been cleaning. That was another good thing about this job. She could get lost in thought and still finish in the proper amount of time. There was so much to do, and she had a lot to think about. It worked out.

"Coming, Pearl," Marlie called back. She hurried downstairs as fast as she dared. As her pregnancy developed, she was becoming more and more cautious of the stairs.

Pearl's eyes went right to her tummy. "I didn't realize you were starting to show so much, Marlie. Ben's going to get crochety about it, I fear."

"I can't help it," Marlie said. "Maybe if I had some proper-fitting clothes, it wouldn't be so obvious. I get stared at every time I leave the inn. I know people want to hear my story ... why I'm expecting a baby with no husband in sight." She sighed.

"I'm sorry, child. The Bible tells us not to judge, but I fear we fall short of that a lot of the time. Single women expecting a wee one aren't that common in our community. It's just the way it is," Pearl explained. "But I am sorry you're uncomfortable. And I apologize for my friends."

"Thank you." Marlie bit her lip. "Anyway, did you need something specific?"

"I do, *jah*," Pearl added. "I wanted to know your due date, so that I can plan out your work accordingly for the next few months. I don't want to give you anything that's going to make you uncomfortable."

"Would it be helpful if I came to you and told you what's making me uncomfortable as time goes on? I really think I'm going to be just fine. I haven't been sick at all," Marlie interjected.

"Climbing up and down the stairs might become a challenge during the later months. Would the kitchen be good for you, if you had some rest time built-in?"

"That would work nicely. I'll talk to you if it doesn't." Marlie offered, although she doubted if she really would tell Pearl. She was still so grateful for her job and for a place to live, that she wasn't about to mess anything up. She wanted to assure Pearl that she could work normally while pregnant for as long as possible.

"Sounds fine," said Pearl. She gave Marlie an affectionate look. "And child, we'll be taking care of the clothing issue right away. Don't fret."

"Thank you, Pearl." Marlie fidgeted with the edge of her apron. "There is one more thing I'm worried about. It's about later ... after the baby is born. Uh, what will I do with the baby while I work? And I'm wondering if Ben will be upset having a crying baby around..."

"We'll work it out," Pearl said. "Don't borrow trouble, as my *mamm* always used to tell me."

Marlie nodded, but in truth, Pearl's words of wisdom did little to console her.

Pearl patted her hand. "If you'll excuse me, I should be going. I have other things I need to be attending to."

"All right. Thank you, Pearl."

Before Marlie returned upstairs, she heard a loud, unusual lowing coming from the barn. She stepped to the window, but she couldn't see anything in particular going on. But the lowing continued, and it sent chills through her. Something was wrong. She turned around and went for her coat and then dashed outside to see if she could help with whatever the problem was.

Abel stood in the yard, talking animatedly to Ben, as another pained lowing sounded. The two of them were so deep in conversation that they hadn't seen her. Marlie held back, watching them.

Then Abel entered the barn, and Ben followed. Marlie crossed to the barn and stood at the door, peering inside. The plaintive lowing that still came from one of the cows stung her ears. The animal was in pain, that was clear. Marlie pressed her hand to her mouth in sympathy. Poor thing.

She stepped inside the barn, watching as the men pulled a cow from its stall. Marlie stepped forward.

"Can I help?" she cried, her heart breaking for the cow's suffering.

Abel looked up. "*Nee.* Stand back, Marlie."

She stood back. He pulled at the rope around the cow's neck, and Ben pushed with his shoulder against the cow's rump. Both men were grunting with exertion as the cow slowly inched forward.

"We have to get her outside into the corral," Ben said, panting.

"We'll make it," Abel said. He rubbed the cow's forehead, talking softly to her as he continued to yank on the lead rope.

Tears stung Marlie's eyes as she watched. Poor thing. Poor, poor thing. What could be wrong with her? She looked to be having trouble walking.

"I didn't see it," Ben said in a voice heavy with regret. Marlie had never heard that tone in his voice before, and her heart went out to him, too.

She watched as slowly they got the cow outside away from the other two cows. She ran ahead and opened the corral gate, then stood back again.

"Thanks," grunted Abel. They got the cow inside and shut the gate.

"What's the matter with her? Will she be all right?"

"Thrush," Abel said.

Marlie had never heard of it.

"I'll get the bleach. Hopefully, the case isn't too far advanced." Ben took off his hat and wiped his sweaty brow. "I can't believe I never saw it."

"Don't be too hard on yourself, *Onkel*," Abel said. "I never saw it either."

"Bleach?" Marlie said.

Ben hurried off, and Abel turned to look at her. "We can treat thrush with a mixture of water and plain old bleach. It usually works."

Marlie stepped up to the coral gate and reached through the slats to pat the cow's neck. "Poor thing," she said. "I'm so sorry for you."

Abel watched her with a strange look of tenderness on his face. She blanched a bit when she saw it, feeling suddenly exposed.

"You're a *gut* person, Marlie," he said, his voice thick. "I'm glad you're here to help Pearl."

Marlie shook her head. "No. It's more like she's helping me." Her hands went to her belly.

Abel's eyes followed the movement, but then he shifted his

gaze back to her eyes. "*Nee.* I stand by my first thought. I'm glad you're here to help Pearl."

Marlie swallowed hard. It was the highest praise she ever remembered receiving.

Chapter Nine

As Marlie went to the kitchen, her mind kept going over and over the gentleness she'd witnessed in Abel as he tended the cow. She wasn't sure if she'd ever seen such gentleness in a man. She'd certainly never seen it in Grant. Nor her father.

Whenever anyone in her family had gotten sick, her father would yell at them to snap out of it. She remembered once when she had a horrendous cough. Even with cough syrup, she couldn't control it. At night, she lay in bed, coughing and coughing. When she couldn't control it, her father was enraged. So all night long, she'd smashed her face into the pillow every time she had to cough, nearly suffocating herself. She'd never forgotten that horrible feeling.

Her eyes misted over with tears as she wondered how Abel

would have handled that situation. He wouldn't have yelled; she was certain of that.

She took out the dinner plates to set the table for supper. There were so many things she was observing and learning during her time there at the inn. More and more, she was drawn to the Amish way of life. It wasn't perfect—she knew that. But there was something about it, something that, despite its imperfections, drew her.

She wanted to take instruction. Wanted to learn more. Wanted to raise her baby in such a community.

She turned on the gas burner to put on the kettle. She could make some nice hot tea for both Ben and Abel when they returned. She'd learned from Pearl that tea soothed nearly everything, and she thought it'd be a nice gesture on her part if she had it ready for the men.

There was a sudden searing pain on her hand.

"Ouch!" she cried, yanking her hand away from the gas flame.

"Here, let me help you with that," a voice said behind her. She turned and found Abel turning on the tap full blast. "Put your hand under here. Quick. It's nice and cold. It'll help."

She did as instructed, and the cool water instantly made her hand feel better. He was standing close to her—so close that she could inhale his scent. She tried to not be affected by his nearness. Tried not to notice his every breath, his every expression. But it was no good.

She liked him. *More* than liked him.

Plain and simple.

The realization made her cheeks go hot. She kept her eyes down so he wouldn't see the truth in her eyes.

"Better?" he asked.

She nodded, still keeping her gaze down.

"I can get you some ice out of the deep freeze."

"*Nee*. I think it'll be fine. I didn't burn it too badly."

He drew her hand out from under the water and inspected it. His touch sent chills through her. She knew she should pull her hand away from his grasp, but she didn't. She let her hand rest in his, and the silence between them thickened.

Finally, it dawned on Marlie that the water was still running. She reached over with her other hand and turned it off.

Abel blinked. "Uh. Right. *Gut*. I'm glad it's better." He let go of her. "I need to go back out. By now, I'm sure Ben has the treatment ready."

"So, you think the cow will be all right? I've never heard such lowing before in my life." She gave a nervous laugh. "Not that I've heard a lot of cows in my life."

He seemed in a hurry to leave. "I reckon so. You be careful now, Marlie."

And with that, he left the kitchen. The kettle of water was whistling now as she hadn't turned off the burner. She flipped it off and filled two cups with steaming water. She plopped a teabag and a spoonful of honey in each cup. They should be nicely steeped when the men came back in.

And then she went to get some ice for her hand herself. It still stung.

Ben walked into the kitchen shortly afterward.

"I'll go tell my *fraa* that you have a burn. Abel told me." He gazed at the two cups of tea.

"I made tea for both you and Abel," she said. "I thought you might appreciate it after seeing to the cow."

His harsh expression softened. Marlie's eyes widened with surprise. Was it possible that he was pleased with her? At least a little?

He gave her a grunt of thanks and picked up the cup of tea. He took a drink and then carried it out of the room with him. Within minutes, Pearl was there.

"*Ach*, child. Ben told me you burned your hand. Let me have a look at it."

Pearl came around and stood in front of her with ointment in her hand. Marlie dropped the ice she'd been pressing on the burn into the sink.

Pearl inspected her skin. "It'll hurt for a day or two, that's for sure and for certain" she said, clucking her tongue. And then she proceeded to gently spreading ointment on it.

Chapter Ten

The weeks and months passed quickly for Marlie. She and Pearl and Ben settled into a quiet rhythm as they all went about their tasks. Marlie and Ben worked out a kind of truce between them, much to Marlie's relief.

The town physician put her due date in mid-to-late February, and Marlie found herself both eager and anxious as February began. In truth, the prospect of the coming birth scared Marlie. She wondered whether she'd have a Valentine's Day baby, and the thought didn't please her. Somehow, the idea of bringing a baby into the world with no father, and her having no husband, was disheartening—especially on the most romantic day of the year. Not that Marlie regretted losing Grant; she'd gotten over that months before, knowing that her life was better without him.

But still ... having a baby alone? Her mind flitted to Abel. He'd become more and more precious to her every week, and he seemed to seek her company out every chance he got. There were times when she could actually feel the affection growing between them. Sometimes, she imagined she saw love in his eyes. She wondered what he saw reflected in her eyes, because she was falling in love with him.

But she couldn't imagine him wanting to take on another man's child. And then there was the whole issue of her taking instruction. Pearl had told her that instruction was traditionally given during the fall, with young people joining church directly afterward.

Marlie didn't want to wait until fall to take instruction, but she didn't figure she had any say in the matter. She looked down at her swollen belly. She wished her child could be born after she'd joined church, but it wasn't to be. She closed her eyes and prayed for patience and wisdom.

She was praying a lot these days, and now, she knew there was a God who listened to her. Praying brought her much comfort during the nights when she couldn't get comfortable enough to sleep more than a couple of hours at a time.

"Are you going to do anything for Valentine's Day?" she asked Pearl one morning during the week before Valentine's Day.

"We don't celebrate Valentine's Day too much," Pearl replied. "However, there might be some heart-shaped boxes of candy floating around as gifts. Still, I'm going to prepare a special dinner for the guests that night, since there will be a couple of newlywed couples at the inn."

A flash of jealousy pricked Marlie, but she ignored it.

"Would you like my help with the meal?" Marlie offered.

"I would, if you feel up to it. *Denke,* Marlie," Pearl said. "Abel has offered his help, too. Although, I ain't used to much help from the men when it comes to putting on a meal." She chuckled.

Pearl looked at Marlie closely and continued, "I have noted that you spend a lot of time with him." She raised a brow while continuing to stir a steaming pot at the cook stove. "I daresay you two have been unofficially courting since you met. We may as well call it what it is."

"Oh, I don't know about that," Marlie said, feeling suddenly embarrassed. But at Pearl's look of consternation, she sighed. "You're right, of course. But I don't want to call it that. I don't want Abel getting in trouble."

Pearl continued to watch her. "Be that as it may... There's no escaping what *Gott* has planned for you, child. The way you two are around each other, I don't think it was sheer luck that Abel was put on temporary lay-off just days after you arrived here."

Marlie felt her cheeks grow warm. Could it be true? Could God have orchestrated this? She had no idea, but the thought warmed her heart. "Perhaps. It's ... an interesting thought."

At that moment, the baby kicked inside her, and Marlie wondered whether the child was agreeing.

The day before Valentine's Day, Pearl left Marlie and Abel to mind the inn since she and Ben had to go into the city for supplies—which would take nearly all day. Marlie felt awkward around Abel as she waddled about the kitchen, preparing a light noon meal. Thank goodness, he soon left the kitchen and went out to work in the barn.

Marlie tasted the gravy. She had been cooking for the guests at the inn for some weeks now as Pearl had taken over all the cleaning. Marlie found that she quite liked to cook.

"You don't need to be going up and down them stairs. Or leaning over the tubs and toilets," Pearl had admonished her when she'd switched up the tasks.

Even though Marlie's feet were swelling, and she had to sit down between stirring pots on the stove, she deeply enjoyed the cooking job.

"Are you doing all right in here, Marlie?" Abel popped in an hour before the noon meal was to be served. "Do you want some help?"

"I'm all right," she said with a smile. "I'll have an hour to get off my feet and let them recuperate after this meal is over. And then later, once I make supper and clean up, I'm done for the day. Pearl's orders."

"*Gut.* I agree with Pearl."

She waved her hand in a friendly dismissal, and with a grin, he left the kitchen.

Her heart pounded hard against her chest as he walked away. She continually marveled at her reactions to his presence. Being around him always gave her a feeling that everything would be all right. She prayed it was true.

She took in a deep breath. She felt every minute of being eight and a half months pregnant. Perhaps, she could get off working at the Valentine's Day dinner—except she'd already promised her help. The pain in her lower back warned her that perhaps she had spoken out of turn. All she really wanted to do was go lie down for a week or two.

Still, helping put with the special meal would be a good way to keep busy. Pearl had an elaborate idea for the dinner, and it would require someone being in the kitchen all day. Pearl had offered to take care of most of the pre-dinner preparations to be done outside of the normal dinner preparation hours, but it didn't make sense to put all the tasks onto Pearl all day.

"The meal is served," Marlie called out once she had finished preparing the current meal. The five current guests had been loitering about the dining room and were more than ready to eat. As the line formed beside the serving counter, Marlie set all the pots and pans of food on the counter.

"Be careful, they're hot," she warned.

She was given many thanks as the guests walked through the line. Their praise made Marlie feel warm and proud. She had learned a lot about meal preparation during her time there, and now, she could even bake loaves of bread from scratch.

She watched everyone help themselves, while she sat contentedly on a corner chair.

"This smells amazing, Marlie," a young mother commented. "But I hope you didn't overdo it on your feet. You look absolutely ready to burst."

Marlie smiled. "I *feel* ready to burst, but I'm not quite there yet. Another week or so, and then I'll have the *boppli*."

She enjoyed talking to the woman. Nearly the same conversation was repeated with each guest. She braced herself for a long, lengthy hour of meal chatting while she rested her feet.

"Smells *gut*, Marlie," Abel said as he came through the end of the line. She'd been looking for him and was glad he'd showed up. "Are you going to be okay later with supper all by yourself?"

"If I need help, you'll be the first one to know," she replied.

Abel went through the line commenting appreciatively about each selection. After he'd gone through, she resisted the urge to close her eyes and take a cat nap. How would that look to the guests? She grimaced. Only a week or two more. That was all.

And then she would be raising a *boppli* without a man to help her.

The thought would not leave her alone. In all honesty, though, she would rather be a single mother than be stuck with someone who was abusive like Grant. Besides, did she need a man at her side to be a good mother...?

She looked at the clock and saw that it had taken less time than she'd thought for everyone to be served. She had about twenty more minutes to relax before she cleaned it all away.

Chapter Eleven

Later, Marlie did end up needing Abel's help to prepare the evening supper. She could barely move her feet, and it hurt to walk. She couldn't do it all alone.

Abel didn't seem to mind in the least. Instead, he happily helped her do what needed to be done. There was something about the way he assisted with no issues or qualms, that made Marlie feel warm inside. Even cared for, and dare she say it ... loved.

As they worked, she couldn't help but keep glancing at him. She giggled more than once at the look of concentration on his face when he was measuring out ingredients. He teased her, too, and the mood inside the kitchen was light and happy, despite the pain in Marlie's feet and lower back.

"Marlie?" Abel's voice had turned serious.

"*Jah?*"

"I want to court you." He took a deep breath. "This isn't meant to be another chance for you to tell me you're not interested, because I think you are. Now, I don't mean to pressure you. I simply want to state my intentions, in addition to the fact that I'm willing to wait for you. You've told me you want to take instruction and join church. After that, there will be no roadblocks for us. But if you want to get settled first after having the *boppli*, that's fine."

She couldn't breathe. She clasped her hands together. He'd said it. He'd told her right out that he wanted to court her. Her mind spun and she felt dizzy.

She looked at him and still had trouble breathing. "I, well, I... Oh, Abel." Tears stung her eyes. "I... There are so many things to think on right now..."

She heard her own words and wondered where they came from. She loved him. Why was she hesitating? Why wasn't she throwing her arms around him and saying yes, yes, yes?

He touched her arm. "I mean it when I say I'll wait, Marlie. I'll wait forever if I have to."

She gazed at him, the tears burning her eyes.

"But," he whispered, "please don't make me wait forever."

She gave him a wobbly smile and nodded, not trusting herself to speak. He smiled back at her then, a smile of pure promise. His eyes shone as he turned to continue preparing the food. She finally was able to draw a breath. Her heart continued to race, but a wonderful peace settled over her.

It could happen. She and Abel. It *could happen.*

Abel continued being a huge help with the food. Marlie couldn't do it without him. Finally, she gave up and let him work alone. He gave her a concerned look as she sank onto a chair.

"If you need me to go get reinforcements, I would be all right with that," he said. "Would you like me to? Or I can keep doing it all myself if you'll keep telling me what to do."

"*Nee.* No one else. I think we'll be all right for now."

"You sit down for as long as you like. In truth, I think it would be more beneficial for you to go lie down until supper and let me and someone else take care of this," Abel urged.

Maybe, he was right. "Are you sure?" she asked. She was feeling worse.

"*Jah.* Please, Marlie," he replied. "You need some rest, and I think it would help you if you put your legs up for a little while. Go take a nap, rest. I'll come get you for dinner." He smiled at her.

"But who will tell you what to do?" She couldn't help but smile.

"I'll find someone. There's that guest, Mrs. Randers. I'm quite sure she'll help me."

"All right. I'll take a rest, then," she said slowly. She took a deep breath. "*Denke.*"

In her room, Marlie did manage to fall asleep for a good couple of hours. As promised, Abel came and woke her for dinner, even though it wasn't all that conventional for an Amish man to come alone to a woman's room. He carried a tray brimming with food, however, insisting that she stay in her room to eat.

She was relieved to eat in her room, and afterward, Mrs. Randers took her dishes back to the kitchen. Marlie felt like she was shirking her duties, though, and ended up meandering down to the lobby later to check on things.

She stepped into the vacant lobby and stopped. Something felt … off. There was something going on in her belly. Pain clenched her lower back, and she knew. It was time. The baby was coming.

She looked frantically around the room, her eyes wide, looking for someone to help her. Someone, *anyone*. But no one was around. Where had everyone gone?

"Marlie? I thought I told you to stay in your r… Are you all right?" Abel frowned., walking toward her. "Marlie?"

"I think the baby—the baby is coming…" The pain in her back was intensifying.

Abel said something about the local medicine woman or something to that effect. Marlie's brain was in a fog… She could think of nothing but the pain.

Abel rushed forward to put his arm around her shoulders. "Come on. Let's get you sitting down at least."

She groaned at a sharp pain, and then, just as quickly, the pain stopped. "Wait," she said. "It's gone."

Abel frowned. "That's how it is supposed to be, ain't it? The pains come and go."

"I don't know," she snapped. "I've never done this before!"

He flinched, and she grabbed his arm.

"I'm sorry," she said. "I'm sorry. That was rude."

"It's all right. Don't worry about it. Shall I get someone?" His brow creased with worry. "Someone to help?"

"Can we wait a little bit? It's gone. Truly. Like, really gone. If it happens again, then yes. Get someone."

One hour later, it became clear that Marlie was not in true labor.

"All right, Marlie," Abel said, standing up from the chair beside hers. "Let's get you back to your bed. You can rest better there."

"No. *Nee.* I want to sit here with you. Just a bit longer. Is that all right?"

"Of course, it is." He smiled at her so tenderly that her heart twisted inside her.

Marlie closed her eyes for a minute, feeling her baby kick restlessly. *Soon,* she thought. *Maybe not today, but soon.* Marlie loved the way Abel had helped her—so tenderly and with such compassion. She wanted that. She wanted that for the rest of her life. And she wanted to do the same for him, too—care for him, love him.

She wanted to be with him forever. As an Amish woman, as his Amish wife.

"Marlie?" he said again, and she opened her eyes. "I love you."

She drew in a quick breath. "And I love you."

He cupped her face in his hands and she felt the rough callouses on his skin. He leaned over and kissed her mouth gently, his lips a mere whisper on hers. "Marry me," he whispered, close to her lips.

"As soon as I can," she whispered back.

He beamed then, kissing her on the cheek. He stood. "Now. Now, let me to help you back to your room. You need to be lying down, Marlie." He hoisted her up, and she leaned heavily on him as they made their way up to her room.

"I will go talk to the bishop tomorrow and see if we can do anything to speed the instruction process up," he told her. "Ideally, I would love the *boppli* to have a father when it comes into the world, but I don't think there will be enough time for that." He chuckled. "But as soon as possible afterward."

Once Marlie was safely settled in bed, he kissed her forehead and started out of the room. "I'm going to sit in the hallway," he told her. "Just in case you need me."

She smiled and closed her eyes, falling asleep almost immediately.

"Marlie?"

Marlie softly groaned.

"Are you asleep?" It was Pearl.

"*Nee*... I'm awake," she said, struggling to sit up. "Did you need something? Did I forget to put something away?"

"*Ach*, child. I wouldn't be fussing with something like that. Abel told me you had some pains."

"I did. But they're gone now."

Pearl nodded. "It happens sometimes. You all right?"

"I'm feeling better. Thanks."

"I've put the kettle on. I'll have some tea for you right quick. Abel told me your plans together. Is it true?" Pearl stepped closer.

Marlie nodded and then noticed Ben standing in the doorway behind Pearl.

He cleared his throat. "Well, I reckon that's *gut* news, then." His voice was gruff, but Marlie heard a note of tenderness hidden in there somewhere.

She told them everything that she and Abel had discussed. The older couple completely understood Abel's urgency and why he would ask for special consideration from the bishop.

"I wanted to be baptized and married to Abel before the *boppli* comes," she said. "But that seems out of the question."

Both Pearl and Ben nodded. Then Pearl stepped forward and put her hand on Marlie's shoulder. "I'm pleased as punch to be welcoming you to the community, child."

Marlie's throat tightened.

"I know it's been a bit of a journey for you," Pearl continued. "And it ain't been easy. Least ways, not a lot of it. But you're here now, and you're staying. *Gott* does his work, child. Haven't I been telling you that all along?"

Marlie nodded. "*Jah*," she murmured. "*Gott* does his work."

"Now, I'll run get that tea," she said, stepping away. She

turned and left the room, leaving Ben still standing in the doorway, looking at Marlie.

Marlie gazed back, not knowing what to say.

Abruptly, Ben coughed. "I'm glad to welcome you, too," he said grumpily and left.

Marlie smiled and closed her eyes.

Chapter Twelve

Four Months Later

Marlie sat in the rocking chair in her room. Abel was on the bed, pulling his shoes on. They had been married for three months. In her arms, Marlie held little Martha Valentine Yoder, her beautiful *dochder* who had been born on Valentine's Day.

"I'll be back late tonight, Marlie," Abel interrupted her thoughts. "Ben has me going down to Hollybrook to look at a new plow blade."

"All right," she replied, smiling. "We'll miss you today."

She walked over and handed baby Martha to him. "What would we do without you?" she said to him softly.

"I don't know." He looked up and smiled. "But I also don't know what I would do without you. Without you *and* our *dochder*."

"I was thinking about when I first received the news that I was pregnant. I was so confused and afraid. I was in a daze, and I couldn't imagine how things would ever work out. I can't help but think I was given Martha so I would end up here, with you, and with a people who have now accepted me as one of their own. And quicker than I ever thought possible."

"That's what happens when you let *Gott* take over your life, Marlie," Abel said seriously. "I wouldn't trade meeting you for anything, and I wouldn't trade having you as my *fraa* for anything, either."

Marlie leaned down and first kissed her daughter's fuzzy head and then kissed Abel.

"We have so much to be thankful for," Abel said, his voice catching. Then he stood. "But I must get going, or I'll be late. *Gut*-bye, Marlie. Bye, wee Martha." He kissed Martha's cheek before handing her back to Marlie.

Marlie watched from the inn's window as he walked out to the buggy. She was glad they were spending their first year of marriage with Pearl and Ben. There was nowhere she'd rather be. She looked down at Martha. The little girl had fallen asleep in her arms. Marlie smiled and put Martha in the crib Ben had made the crib for her in a matter of a weekend. And once they had let everyone know the wedding was happening, gifts of love and acceptance had poured in.

"You don't know how lucky we are, Martha," Marlie whispered. "You get to grow up with a loving father. I didn't have such a luxury when I was young. Enjoy it, for the love of a *daed* is a true blessing."

She roused a smile from the little girl and retreated back to the rocking chair. Life had taken on a new richness after she'd given birth.

Over the last month, Marlie had started learning how to sew. She took to doing it while Martha napped. And if she needed help with one of her sewing projects, she could always get Pearl and let her hold Martha while she sewed.

There was a knock at the door. She set her sewing down. Though she wanted to finish the dress, she was afraid another knock would wake little Martha up. When she opened the door, she was pleased to find Pearl standing on the other side.

"If you're hoping to hold Martha, she's already asleep," Marlie told her with a smile. She opened the door a little wider. "But come on in. We can whisper."

"I came to see if you needed any help with that dress of yours.

I know you like to sew while the *boppli* sleeps." Pearl walked into the room. "Has Abel already left?"

"*Jah*. You just missed him."

"Where is the dress?"

"On the bed," Marlie said and pointed toward it. Their voices remained lowered as Pearl helped Marlie set in the sleeves. Marlie had tried to get them right on her own, but she had gathered them too much and couldn't figure out how to take out just the right amount so they would lay properly.

Once the sleeves were firmly attached, the dress was well on its way to being finished.

"That looks beautiful for a first try," Pearl complimented her. "Try it on."

Even though the hem wasn't in, Marlie decided to try it on anyway. She slipped into the bathroom and came out with the dress on, beaming.

"I don't think I've ever seen you smile so widely before," Pearl said. "You look beautiful in that dress."

"*Denke*," Marlie said with pride. She gave Pearl a hug. "I've never felt happy, safe, *and* content at the same time... And Pearl, so much of that is thanks to you."

Pearl's eyes misted over, and she looked embarrassed. "Nonsense. *Gott* did it."

"Through you, Pearl," Marlie said, her voice choking up. "Through you."

"That's how love is supposed to work, dear," Pearl said, hugging her back.

Marlie gazed at the older woman and then glanced at her tiny, perfect little baby, lying so peacefully in her crib—her little chest rising and falling with her soft breaths.

"*Jah*," Marlie agreed. "That's exactly how love is supposed to work."

The End

Continue Reading...

❦

Thank you for reading **Marlie's Awakening! Are you wondering what to read next?** Why not read one of Brenda Maxfield's Amish romances? **Here's a peek of *The Mother's Helper* for you:**

Nancy Slagel cradled the baby in her arms. She felt the sting of tears pushing against her eyelids and held the child closer. Why couldn't this child be hers? She was twenty-one, plenty old enough.

If only Mark hadn't...

She shuddered. She couldn't let her mind wander down that road. She just *couldn't*. She was sick to death of tears.

But why had he done it? And with her own *sister*? Her father had tried to make excuses for Susan. "She's always been so tender-hearted," he told her. "When Mark was hurt, and you were gone ... well, it was a work of the Lord *Gott*."

Really? Having her beau stolen by her own sister had been *God's work*? Hardly. And it wasn't like Nancy would have been gone for good. She'd been away for one night visiting her grandmother. *One night!* It just couldn't have been so simple. Susan must have had designs on Mark from the start.

And Mark? To be able to deflect that easily?

It didn't bear thinking about.

Nancy cuddled the sleeping babe. If it didn't bear thinking about, then why did her mind continually go there? Why did she torture herself with thoughts of Mark's betrayal? She blinked hard, willing her tears not to fall. Nobody wanted to be around a cry-baby. Especially when that cry-baby was twenty-one years old. In truth, Nancy was beginning to detest herself for her continual weeping.

If only she could stop it...

"Nancy?" her cousin Irene tiptoed into the room. "He asleep?"

"*Jah*." Nancy kissed the fluffy hair on top of the baby's head. "Shall I put him down?"

"Go ahead. He should sleep for a while now."

Nancy moved gracefully to the crib and lowered the child to the mattress. Zeke stirred, but only for a second. Then he put his thumb in his mouth and sucked earnestly, his eyes still closed.

The two cousins tip-toed out of the room.

"You need to rest," Nancy said. "Go on, now. I'll start supper. Where's Debbie?"

Irene yawned and rolled her shoulders as if they were paining her. "She's downstairs playing with her blocks. I shouldn't leave her for more than a second or two."

Nancy put her hand on Irene's arm. "I'm going down. You get a nap in while you can."

"A nap? It just don't seem right when there's so much to do."

"Irene," Nancy scolded her, "that's the reason for a mother's helper. Now, let me earn my keep."

Irene smiled, stifling another yawn. "All right. But I won't sleep long."

"Sleep as long as you like." Nancy smiled and slipped out of the room. She hurried downstairs and went immediately to the front room to check on Debbie.

The two-year-old was rolling on the floor, her arms stretched wide. The blocks were strewn all over the rag rug.

Nancy squatted down next to her. "Come on, Debbie. Want to help me work on supper?"

"*Jah!*" Debbie said with a giggle. She got right up and toddled toward the kitchen. Nancy laughed and followed her.

VISIT HERE To Read More:

http://ticahousepublishing.com/amish.html

Thank you for Reading

If you **love Amish Romance**, **Visit Here:**

http://ticahousepublishing.subscribemenow.com

to find out about all **New Hannah Miller Amish Romance Releases! We will let you know as soon as they become available!**

If you enjoyed *Marlie's Awakening* would you kindly take a couple minutes to leave a positive review on Amazon? It only takes a moment, and positive reviews truly make a difference. I would be so grateful! Thank you!

Turn the page to discover more Hannah Miller Amish Romances just for you!

More Amish Romance from Hannah Miller

Waiting for Jake is Coming Soon!

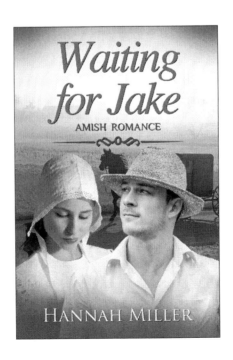

About the Author

Hannah Miller has been writing Amish Romance for the past seven years. Long intrigued by the Amish way of life, Hannah has traveled the United States, visiting different Amish communities. She treasures her Amish friends and enjoys visiting with them. Hannah makes her home in Indiana, along with her husband, Robert. Together, they have three children and seven grandchildren. Hannah loves to ride bikes in the sunshine. And if it's warm enough for a picnic, you'll find her under the nearest tree!

Made in the USA
Lexington, KY
07 July 2019